little Miss Greedy

by Roger Hargreaves

Little Miss Greedy certainly was.

What?

Greedy!

I'll say.
As greedy as a giant!
And giants are really very greedy indeed.

Little Miss Greedy lived in Cherrycake Cottage.

One lovely summer morning, a Monday,
Little Miss Greedy awoke earlier than usual.

She felt rather hungry, and so she went
into her kitchen and cooked herself
some breakfast.

Some breakfast indeed!

Sausages!

Now if you had sausages for breakfast,
or if I had sausages for breakfast,
how many sausages would we have?

One?
Perhaps two?
Maybe three?

Guess how many sausages Little Miss Greedy
had for breakfast.

Sixty-six!

Go on, count them!

Sixty-six succulent, sizzling sausages.

Which is difficult to say.

And even more difficult to eat.

Unless you're Little Miss Greedy!

Little Miss Greedy cut the last sausage on her plate in two, and popped one half into her mouth.

"Mmm!" she sighed, contentedly.
"That was nice," she thought to herself.
"Now what else shall I have?"

Guess what?

Toast!

Now if you had toast for breakfast,
or if I had toast for breakfast,
how many slices would we have?

Perhaps two?
Maybe three?

Guess how many slices of toast
Little Miss Greedy had for breakfast.

Twenty-three!
Twenty-three thick, tasty slices of tempting toast!
And marmalade.

Just as Little Miss Greedy was licking
the last crumb of the twenty-third slice
of toast from her lips, there was a knock
at the door of Cherrycake Cottage.

It was the postman.

"Letter for you, Little Miss Greedy," he said,
cheerfully.

"Oh good," smiled Little Miss Greedy,
for she liked it when someone sent her a letter.

"Would you like a cup of tea while you're here?"
she asked. "I'm going to have one."

One indeed!

Just look at the size of Little Miss Greedy's teapot!

The postman had one cup of tea and a chat, thanked Little Miss Greedy, and left.

Little Miss Greedy poured herself another cup (another after the eleven other cups she'd already had) and opened her letter.

It was from her cousin, Mr Greedy.

'Dear Little Miss Greedy,' he had written.
(He always wrote to his cousin this way.)

'Next Wednesday is my birthday.
Please come to tea at 4 o'clock.'

Little Miss Greedy was delighted.

She hadn't seen her cousin for
quite some time.

Wednesday was a lovely day.

After a little light lunch (I'll tell you what later),
Little Miss Greedy set off in her car to drive
to Mr Greedy's house.

But before she set off, she put something on
the back seat of her car.

Something large.

Mr Greedy's birthday present.

At 4 o'clock precisely, Little Miss Greedy
pulled up in front of Mr Greedy's roly-poly
sort of a house.

Mr Greedy was there to meet her.

"Hello, Little Miss Greedy," he smiled.
"How lovely to see you after all this time!"

"Happy birthday," laughed Little Miss Greedy,
and she gave Mr Greedy a big kiss.

Mr Greedy blushed.

"Do come in," he said. "Tea's all ready!"

Little Miss Greedy was following Mr Greedy into
his house when she remembered something.
You know what it was, don't you?
That's right.
Mr Greedy's birthday present!

"Wait a minute," she said. "Can you help me to
lift something out of the back of my car, please?"
She smiled.
"It's rather heavy," she added.
"Certainly," agreed Mr Greedy.

There, on the back seat of Little Miss Greedy's car, was the biggest birthday cake you've ever seen in all your life.

A huge, **enormous**, gigantic, colossal currant cake, with thick pink icing on top and strawberry jam in the middle.

"I only put one candle on it," explained Little Miss Greedy as they carried it to the house, "because I've forgotten how old you are!"

"Oh, you shouldn't have," laughed Mr Greedy. He licked his lips. "But I'm glad you did!"

"I baked it today," said Little Miss Greedy.

And then she chuckled.

"I have a confession to make," she said.

"This isn't the only cake I baked today!
The first one looked so delicious,
I ate it for breakfast!"

She chuckled again.

"And the second one looked so delicious,"
she went on,
"I ate that one for my lunch!"

Mr Greedy grinned from ear to ear.

"Time for tea, Little Miss Greedy" he said.

3 Great Offers for MR. MEN Fans!

MR. MEN TOKEN

1 New Mr. Men or Little Miss Library Bus Presentation Cases

A brand new stronger, roomier school bus library box, with sturdy carrying handle and stay-closed fasteners.

The full colour, wipe-clean boxes make a great home for your full collection.

They're just £5.99 inc P&P and free bookmark!

☐ MR. MEN ☐ LITTLE MISS (please tick and order overleaf)

2 Door Hangers and Posters

In every Mr. Men and Little Miss book like this one, you will find a special token. Collect 6 tokens and we will send you a brilliant Mr. Men or Little Miss poster and a Mr. Men or Little Miss double sided full colour bedroom door hanger of your choice. Simply tick your choice in the list and tape a 50p coin for your two items to this page.

PLEASE STICK YOUR 50P COIN HERE

Door Hangers (please tick)
☐ Mr. Nosey & Mr. Muddle
☐ Mr. Slow & Mr. Busy
☐ Mr. Messy & Mr. Quiet
☐ Mr. Perfect & Mr. Forgetful
☐ Little Miss Fun & Little Miss Late
☐ Little Miss Helpful & Little Miss Tidy
☐ Little Miss Busy & Little Miss Brainy
☐ Little Miss Star & Little Miss Fun

Posters (please tick)
☐ MR.MEN
☐ LITTLE MISS

3 Sixteen Beautiful Fridge Magnets – any 2 for £2.00! inc.P&P

They're very special collector's items!
Simply tick your first and second* choices from the list below
of any 2 characters!

1st Choice

- [ ] Mr. Happy
- [ ] Mr. Lazy
- [ ] Mr. Topsy-Turvy
- [ ] Mr. Bounce
- [ ] Mr. Bump
- [ ] Mr. Small
- [ ] Mr. Snow
- [ ] Mr. Wrong

- [ ] Mr. Daydream
- [ ] Mr. Tickle
- [ ] Mr. Greedy
- [ ] Mr. Funny
- [ ] Little Miss Giggles
- [ ] Little Miss Splendid
- [ ] Little Miss Naughty
- [ ] Little Miss Sunshine

2nd Choice

- [ ] Mr. Happy
- [ ] Mr. Lazy
- [ ] Mr. Topsy-Turvy
- [ ] Mr. Bounce
- [ ] Mr. Bump
- [ ] Mr. Small
- [ ] Mr. Snow
- [ ] Mr. Wrong

- [ ] Mr. Daydream
- [ ] Mr. Tickle
- [ ] Mr. Greedy
- [ ] Mr. Funny
- [ ] Little Miss Giggles
- [ ] Little Miss Splendid
- [ ] Little Miss Naughty
- [ ] Little Miss Sunshine

*Only in case your first choice is out of stock.

--- TO BE COMPLETED BY AN ADULT ---

To apply for any of these great offers, ask an adult to complete the coupon below and send it with the appropriate payment and tokens, if needed, to MR. MEN OFFERS, PO BOX 7, MANCHESTER M19 2HD

- [ ] Please send _____ Mr. Men Library case(s) and/or _____ Little Miss Library case(s) at £5.99 each inc P&P
- [ ] Please send a poster and door hanger as selected overleaf. I enclose six tokens plus a 50p coin for P&P
- [ ] Please send me _____ pair(s) of Mr. Men/Little Miss fridge magnets, as selected above at £2.00 inc P&P

Fan's Name _____

Address _____

_____ **Postcode** _____

Date of Birth _____

Name of Parent/Guardian _____

Total amount enclosed £ _____

- [ ] **I enclose a cheque/postal order payable to Egmont Books Limited**
- [ ] **Please charge my MasterCard/Visa/Amex/Switch or Delta account** (delete as appropriate)

Card Number

Expiry date __/__ **Signature** _____

MR.MEN   LITTLE MISS
Mr. Men and Little Miss™ & ©Mrs. Roger Hargreaves

CUT ALONG DOTTED LINE AND RETURN THIS WHOLE PAGE